THE BR
BUS BO
A FIGHT FOR RACIAL JUSTICE

Written by Sandra A. Agard

Illustrated by Chellie Carroll

Contents

Collins

1 INTRODUCTION – THE DREAM

"I have a dream ..." These words were used in a speech by Martin Luther King Junior, who was one of the leaders of the **Civil Rights Movement**. His dream was to end **racism** in the USA so that people would not be judged by the colour of their skin.

FACT!

Martin Luther King Junior gave his famous speech in front of 250,000 people in Washington, D.C., USA.

3

King's powerful speech was given on 28th August 1963. It led to the USA passing two important laws that made it illegal to **discriminate** against someone because of their race.

On that same day, in Bristol, UK, there was another important victory against racism. The Bristol Omnibus Company said that it would stop refusing to give jobs to people because of their race.

a Bristol Omnibus Company bus

This was a victory for a protest organised by six young men who were fighting for everyone to have the same rights. That protest was called the Bristol Bus **Boycott**, and it changed **race relations** and laws in the UK.

This is the story of how it happened.

Three of the Bristol Bus Boycott campaigners: Audley Evans, Paul Stephenson and Owen Henry.

5

2 WELCOME TO BRISTOL

The city of Bristol was the UK's main slave port in the early 1700s.

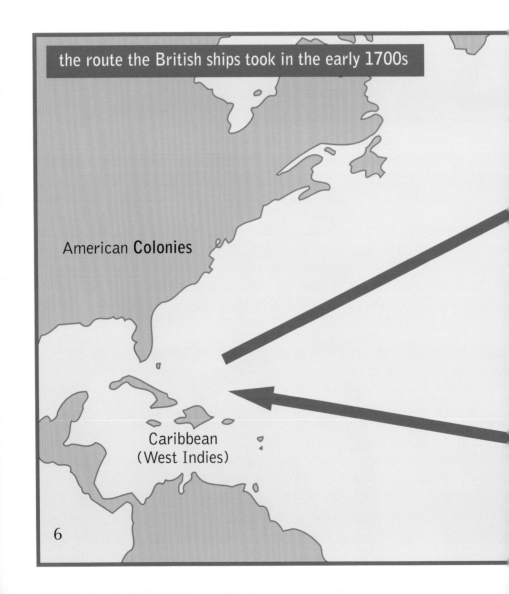

the route the British ships took in the early 1700s

American **Colonies**

Caribbean
(West Indies)

Rich people paid for ships to travel to Africa. The ships were filled with African people who were taken to the Caribbean, which has also often been called the West Indies. There, they were forced to work on sugar and tobacco plantations. Some of the sugar and tobacco was brought back to Bristol and sold there.

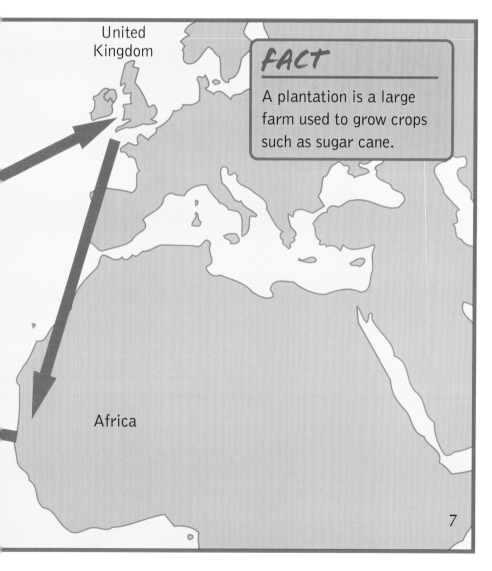

United Kingdom

FACT

A plantation is a large farm used to grow crops such as sugar cane.

Africa

After the damage caused by bombing during the Second World War, the UK needed help to rebuild its cities. In 1947, the British government invited people from across the British Empire and British Commonwealth to come to the UK to work.

men at Bristol unloading sugar from the West Indies

Many people, including thousands from the Caribbean, came to live in the UK. They thought they would have a better life there. Some went to London and some went to other major cities, such as Bristol.

FACT

The British Commonwealth, now known as the Commonwealth, is made up of 54 countries from all over the world.

By the 1960s, there were about 3000 people of Caribbean descent living in Bristol. Some had come because the government had invited them to. Others had fought for the UK in the Second World War and had decided to stay.

They were often treated badly. Some were beaten up by gangs of young White men. Signs saying "No Coloured Men" in the windows of houses meant that the owner would not rent rooms to them.

Even though the new arrivals had been invited to come and work in the UK, they found that many businesses would not give them jobs. This **discrimination** was known as the **colour bar**. It seems shocking now, but there were no laws against it in the 1960s.

FACT

In the 1960s there were no laws against stopping Black people from entering restaurants and bars, or people refusing to give Black people jobs and housing.

3 ON THE BUSES

The Bristol Omnibus Company was one of Bristol's biggest employers and was seen by new arrivals to the city as a key place to apply for jobs.

However, it was also one of many companies that discriminated against Black and Asian people, whom they called "coloured people".

Despite there being a **labour shortage** in the city, they refused to hire anyone who was not White to work on their buses. They only employed Black and Asian people in low-paid positions, such as in the workshops and canteens.

To understand the reason for this, we need to talk about trade unions. A trade union is an organisation that workers join, with the aim of making sure they are paid fairly and treated well by their bosses. The bus workers' union was called the Transport and General Workers' Union or TGWU for short.

In 1955, TGWU members voted on a rule that "coloured" workers should not be employed to work on the buses. They wanted to protect their jobs, fearing that hiring Black people would mean everyone would be paid less.

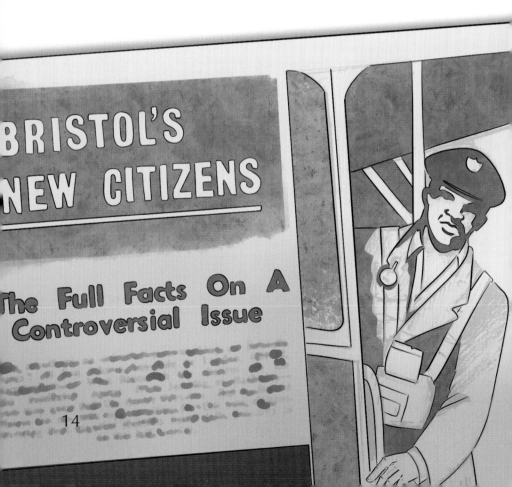

The bus company was also responsible for discrimination against Black people. In 1962, the head of the bus company, Ian Patey, said that the "presence of Black crews would **downgrade** the job and drive existing staff away". This was a common assumption at the time: if Black people did a job then it would be seen as less important and many White people would not want to do it.

NO COLOUR BAR ON OUR BUSES

—but no jobs either for the immigrants

4 A PLAN OF ACTION

A group of young Caribbean men felt that this discrimination had to end.

In 1962, they formed an action group called the West Indian Development Council to campaign for better housing, fairer employment rights and an end to the continual **harassment** of Caribbean people.

This group was made up of Roy Hackett, Owen Henry, Paul Stephenson, Prince Brown and Audley Evans.

FACT

The West Indies is a term used to refer to a group of islands in the Caribbean. These include the islands of Jamaica, Trinidad and Tobago, Barbados, Antigua and Barbuda, as well as Guyana on the mainland in South America. These countries are also part of the Commonwealth.

17

Paul Stephenson, a youth worker, arrived from Essex to join the group and became their **spokesperson**. Together, they decided that more decisive action needed to be taken in order to create change.

The group planned a large protest and drew inspiration from events in Montgomery, Alabama, USA, in 1955.

At that point in time, buses in Alabama were segregated, meaning that White people sat at the front of the bus and Black people sat at the back. If the "Whites Only" section was full, then Black people were required by law to give up their seats for White people.

When African Americans such as Claudette Colvin and Rosa Parks were arrested for refusing to give up their seats for White people, a bus boycott was organised to protest against the injustice. People who supported equality refused to ride on the buses, and the city of Montgomery lost so much money they had no choice but to give in and end **segregation** on their transport network. This was a huge victory in the battle for civil rights in the USA and inspired Martin Luther King Junior to make his famous speech in Washington, D.C.

Rosa Parks

The bus boycott in Montgomery gained a lot of newspaper coverage in the USA.

The Montgomery Advertiser

Bus Desegregation Order Served Here

Negroes Vote To Call Off Boycott Today

5 THE JOB THAT VANISHED

The West Indian Development
Council believed a bus boycott
in Bristol could force the bus
company to change its policies,
but for their boycott to make
an impact they needed a
lot of people to support it.
They decided they needed to
show everyone that the colour
bar existed.

To do this they required
the help of 18-year-old
Guy Bailey.

Guy Bailey had recently
arrived from Jamaica and was
working as a **dispatch clerk** in
a clothing warehouse. However,
he really wanted to work on
the double-decker buses as it
seemed a more exciting career.

22

The Bristol Omnibus Company advertised their vacancies around the city with posters only showing White people.

Paul Stephenson, the spokesperson for the West Indian Development Council, met Guy Bailey through his work as a youth officer. He saw this eager young man as an ideal candidate for a job at the bus company. When an advert appeared asking for new conductors, Stephenson rang the company to arrange a job interview. He saw this as a great chance to show the world the company's unfair hiring policy.

On the day of the interview, Guy put on his best suit and
at 2 o'clock precisely he arrived at the company. He was
not welcomed.

When the receptionist at the front desk told the manager
that a Black man had arrived to be interviewed, the manager
replied, saying "that all of the vacancies had been filled".

Bailey knew this was not true. One of his friends had confirmed there were jobs available just an hour before. Bailey complained and refused to leave. Eventually, the manager told him, "There's no point having an interview. We don't employ Black people."

Paul and the other members of the West Indian Development Council had been proved right. The colour bar did exist within the Bristol Omnibus Company. The time had come to call for a boycott of the buses.

Stephenson held a press conference in his flat in the St Pauls area of Bristol and announced that the bus boycott would begin on 30th April 1963.

He told the press what had happened to Guy Bailey. He also highlighted the experiences of Roy Hackett, who was turned down for a job as a **labourer** by a company who said that they never employed Africans; they could not even be bothered to acknowledge the fact that he was actually from Jamaica in the Caribbean. As well as this, Hackett's wife Ena had been refused employment as a bus conductor, despite meeting all the job requirements. This was clearly the colour bar in action over and over again. These examples shocked a lot of people and made them want to help. The next day, with support from the West Indian community and many of the White people in the city including students and tutors from Bristol University, the Bus Boycott began.

28

6 THE BOYCOTT BEGINS

During the boycott, supporters refused to use the buses. Marches were held all over Bristol and protests were held outside bus depots and along bus routes.

The West Indian Development Council wanted to stop buses getting into the city centre. They organised groups of protesters to go to key areas and stand in the middle of roads holding signs to stop the buses going through. Soon roads were **gridlocked**. The boycott was working.

But this disruption was only part of the plan.
Stephenson invited photographers to follow Owen Henry,
one of the members of the group, on to a Bristol bus;
he stood at the back.

This stunt appealed to the British press as it highlighted
similarities between the treatment of Black people in the UK
and the USA. In both cases, they were fighting segregation.

However, whereas in Alabama Black people were forced to stand at the back of the bus, in Bristol the back of the bus was where the bus conductor would stand, a job the bus company would not allow Black people to do. For Henry, standing at the back was about defying the colour bar.

By drawing parallels with segregation in the USA, the West Indian Development Council wanted to shame authorities into action.

The boycott did have its challenges. At first, not all Caribbean people supported it, fearing they would lose their jobs or be made homeless by their landlords. Even so, a large number of people did support it, and the boycott gathered **momentum**.

Guy Bailey was crucial to the success of the boycott. He was a quiet, dignified and respectable person. This made him ideal to be the public face of the boycott. Many people disapproved of how he had been treated, and public opinion across the country shifted in favour of the boycott.

I thought there was no colour bar, says Guy

7 THE END OF THE COLOUR BAR

The boycott attracted support from a wide variety of places. On 1st May 1963, students from Bristol University held a protest march to the bus station and the local trade union offices.

Many well-known people spoke out in support of the boycott. Politicians such as Anthony Wedgwood Benn and Harold Wilson supported it.

Anthony Wedgwood Benn

The High Commissioner for Trinidad and Tobago, the West Indian cricketer Learie Constantine, along with other diplomats from the Caribbean, publicly criticised the bus company.

Learie Constantine

The boycott even drew the support of another union, the Bristol Trades Council, who publicly criticised the bus workers' union (TGWU) and their support of the bus company.

Our Policy Stays, says bus chief

NO COLOUR BAR ON OUR BUSES

Busmen Heckle Marchers

Despite the increasing pressure, the TGWU refused to meet in person with protesters. Instead, each side put their view across in newspaper articles.

SIR LEARIE JOINS IN COLOUR BAR ISSUE

WEST INDIANS 100% FOR BUS BOYCOTT

WILSON JOINS COLOUR BAR FRAY

The boycott continued for months until the bus company and the TGWU finally gave in to the pressure.

On 27th August 1963, a meeting of 500 bus workers agreed to end the colour bar. A day later, Ian Patey, the head of the Bristol Omnibus Company, announced there would be no more discrimination in employing bus crews.

There was to be "complete integration" in the workforce on the buses, "without regard to race, colour or **creed**".
This was the same day that Martin Luther King Junior made his famous "I Have a Dream" speech in Washington, D.C.

The protesters had won. At the Bristol Omnibus Company the colour bar was finally destroyed.

8 VICTORY

On 17th September 1963, Raghbir Singh, became the first non-White bus conductor in Bristol, and the following year, Norman Samuels became the first Black bus driver in Bristol.

Paul Stephenson argued that the victory over the Bristol Omnibus Company paved the way for the Race Relations Acts of 1965 and 1968. These were new laws that banned discrimination in all public places, housing and employment in the UK.

For a long time, the importance of the Bristol Bus Boycott was forgotten. It took several years for the leaders to get the recognition they deserved.

In 2009, Paul Stephenson, Guy Bailey and Roy Hackett were awarded **OBEs** for their parts in the campaign. But it took another four years before the Transport and General Workers' Union issued an apology for their actions.

In 2014 a commemorative plaque was unveiled at Bristol Bus Station honouring the men who helped to organise the boycott, ensuring their success would not be forgotten.

Finally, in 2017, Paul Stephenson received a Pride of Britain Lifetime Achievement Award.

The organisers of the Bristol Bus Boycott, Paul Stephenson, Roy Hackett, Owen Henry, Guy Bailey, Prince Brown and Audley Evans had made history. Like Martin Luther King Junior, they had a dream. Their dream was to end the colour bar, and they made it a reality.

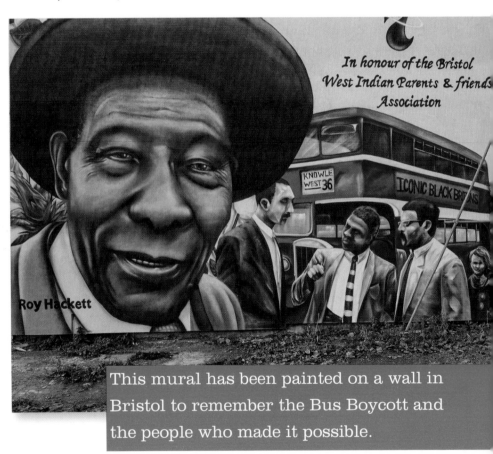

This mural has been painted on a wall in Bristol to remember the Bus Boycott and the people who made it possible.

GLOSSARY

boycott a political and social protest when people decide not to use the buses and block the bus routes, to make a point

Civil Rights Movement the protest movement in the USA that fought for equal rights for Black Americans and against racial segregation and discrimination

colonies countries or areas under the control of another country

colour bar when people of different races are separated and not given the same rights and opportunities

creed a statement of the basic beliefs of a religious faith

discriminate / discrimination the unfair or unjust treatment of certain groups of people

dispatch clerk a person who organises deliveries from a warehouse

downgrade to make something seem less important

gridlocked a traffic jam in which no vehicles can move because key streets are blocked by traffic

harassment offensive or intimidating behaviour

labourer someone employed to do manual (physical) work

labour shortage not enough people to do the jobs that exist

momentum when a protest becomes more popular and successful

OBE (Order of the British Empire) an award given to people in the UK who have achieved great things

racism unjust or unfair treatment based on race/colour of skin

race relations the relationship between different races of people

segregation separation of people due to their skin colour

spokesperson a person who speaks as the representative of a group or an organisation

BRISTOL BUS BOYCOTT TIMELINE

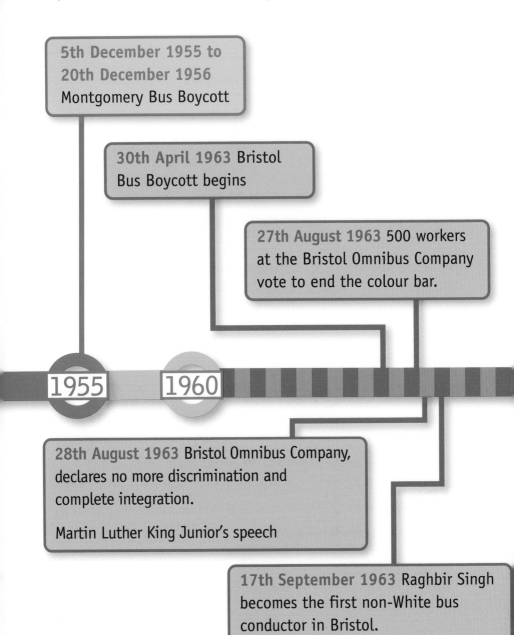

5th December 1955 to 20th December 1956 Montgomery Bus Boycott

30th April 1963 Bristol Bus Boycott begins

27th August 1963 500 workers at the Bristol Omnibus Company vote to end the colour bar.

1955

1960

28th August 1963 Bristol Omnibus Company, declares no more discrimination and complete integration.

Martin Luther King Junior's speech

17th September 1963 Raghbir Singh becomes the first non-White bus conductor in Bristol.

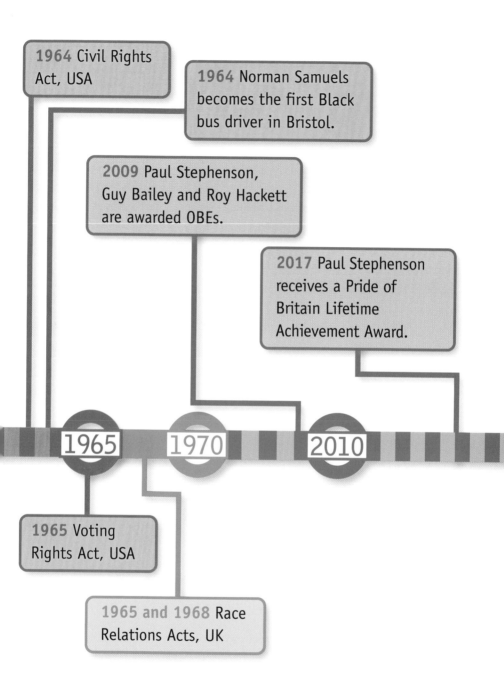

1964 Civil Rights Act, USA

1964 Norman Samuels becomes the first Black bus driver in Bristol.

2009 Paul Stephenson, Guy Bailey and Roy Hackett are awarded OBEs.

2017 Paul Stephenson receives a Pride of Britain Lifetime Achievement Award.

1965

1970

2010

1965 Voting Rights Act, USA

1965 and 1968 Race Relations Acts, UK

 Ideas for reading

Written by Gill Matthews
Primary Literacy Consultant

Reading objectives:

- Read books that are structured in different ways and reading for a range of purposes
- Identify main ideas drawn from more than one paragraph and summarising these
- Participate in discussion about books, taking turns and listening to what others say

Spoken language objectives:

- Articulate and justify answers, arguments and opinions
- Maintain attention and participate actively in collaborative conversations, staying on topic and initiating and responding to comments
- Participate in discussions, presentations, performances, role play, improvisations and debates

Curriculum links: Citizenship – Preparing to play an active role as citizens; Developing good relationships and respecting the differences between people

Interest words: protest march, discrimination, integration, awarded, apology, honouring

Build a context for reading

- Look at the front cover of the book and discuss the title. Explore children's understanding of a boycott.
- Read the back cover blurb and explore the children's responses to the content.
- Ask what children understand by the subtitle *A fight for racial justice*.
- Establish that this is a non-fiction book, written as a recount, and ask children what kinds of features it might contain. Challenge them to find and use the contents page to identify how the book is organised.